# The Kalikantzaroi:

*A Christmas Tale
about the fabled and clever goblins
of Anatolia Greece*

*The story of the mischievous little devils,
known as the Kalikantzaroi*

# The Kalikantzaroi — A Christmas Tale

NIKOS LINARDAKIS

*To:*

———————————————

*From:*

———————————————

# THE KALIKANTZAROI — A CHRISTMAS TALE

©2024 Nikos Linardakis and

NEW EDITION PUBLISHING

All rights reserved.

No part of this publication may be reproduced, stored in a retrieval system, or transmitted in any form or by any means (including electronic, mechanical, photocopying, recording, or otherwise) without prior written permission from the publisher.

ISBN 978-1-884084-14-0

Cover Jacket Design by Victor Hofmeister
VictorHofmeister.com

Manufactured in the United States

First Edition, First Paperback Printing

Story Typeset in Perpetua 14

Book One in the Kalikantzaroi™ Series
By Nikos Linardakis

# The Kalikantzaroi — A Christmas Tale

## Author's Message

Behold, the tale you are about to read
is one woven through the fabric of time, and
handed down from generation to generation.
Now, it comes to you,
retold by a modern-day Greek storyteller,
known to many as "Santa Nikos."

This story is a new retelling—
*The Legend of the Kalikantzaroi.*
After centuries of oral tradition,
I share it with you, as I remember it,
passed down from the remote mountains and
quiet villages of Anatolia, Greece.

It is a fusion of cautionary tales,
filled with mischief and destruction,
yet anchored in a deeper truth:
the enduring triumph of goodness,
resilience, and faith,
even in the shadow of darkness.

May God be with you.

Nikos Linardakis, M.D.
—The Author—

December, 2024
Collierville, TN

# The Kalikantzaroi — A Christmas Tale

# The Backstory

I saw him again this year, on a bitter and late December night. As I looked out my family room window, there he was. That foul creature—hunched on the side porch, oddly resting, and pretending to shiver. A Kalikantzaros, one of the mischievous goblins of Anatolia, Greece (now considered Turkey).

My American friends butcher the name as "Collie-Cancerous," which, to be honest, isn't too far off in pronunciation! This creature, like the others, was putrid and devilish—revolting beyond words. He drooled snot, oozing from his left nostril.

His crooked nose dripped incessantly, and he licked it away—slowly, deliberately—only for more dribble to follow and a stormy, deliberate lick—then, he mocked me with a wicked grin, as if daring me to look away.

He hissed, "I'm Megalomiti, and I've been watching you…" His raspy voice delivered each word in a high pitch, like nails on a chalkboard.

He concealed his eyes with his two soiled and bristly-haired, stubby hands. Then, with a dramatic reveal, he uncovered them, exposing two piercing eyes. The pupils burned fiery-red, encircled by blazing orange iris rings centered against the jaundiced, veiny whites of his eyes.

He threw me a jerky smile—with another crooked, unsettling grin that sent a chill down my spine. His movements were fidgety and neurotic. That awkward smirk only deepened my unease.

"Look," he paused for a still moment, "all I want…," Megalomiti hesitated again, as if making up his next thought, "All I want…is a small glass of carrot juice."

He twitched nervously, and before I could react, the Kalikantzaros jumped over the porch deck, opened the side door, and entered my home! This could have been avoided, but unfortunately, I forgot to lock the door and I left it slightly open.

"Stop!" I shouted, raising my hand to block his path. The goblin paid no attention. I continued to demand that he listen, with all of my five fingers open. "Stop!"

"Wooah, settle down, Fatso!" he sneered. Describing me in a way I knew, but never wanted to hear. He continued, "I'm not here to hurt you. Just give me some carrot juice. You can't drink it all yourself!"

With a swift plunge, the refrigerator door swung open and he guzzled down the entire bottle of carrot juice in less than three seconds. He moved towards me, but then shifted back into the kitchen.

This time, the Kalikantzaros was alone. I didn't see any other ones. My thought was to trap him, but I feared he might give me a disease. At this point, I was concerned for my own safety.

"No, you look—this is my house, and I didn't invite you here. You can leave now." I said, my voice firm and stern as I puffed up my chest and shoulders.

Megalomiti, barely three feet tall, moved quickly. After guzzling the carrot juice, he tossed the glass to the floor. It shattered with a loud crash, scattering shards and creating a slick, dangerous mess.

"That's for not being a gentleman and offering me juice when I asked. You denied it!" he barked, condemning me for his own theft.

Before I could respond, he leapt onto the kitchen countertop, snatched two freshly baked loaves of bread, and jammed them into his mouth, swallowing them whole.

"You were not invited. Please leave, Mr. Megalomiti," I demanded, gesturing him politely toward the door again, my voice was strong, though my heart pounded. Megalomiti just crackled and spat out a foul yellowish-green glob of odorous snot that splattered across my kitchen walls. Without hesitation, he jumped for the doorknob, then turned back to survey his mess. Gooey snot covered the walls, the floor, the counter—even my reading glasses and shirt!

"That's it!" I shouted in fury as I lunged at him, but he was faster. As he fumbled to open the door, I rushed to the kitchen drawer, grabbed a vial of holy water, and splashed it at him. It sizzled on his skin like acid, and he shrieked in agony, feeling the sting burn through his pelt.

Megalomiti bolted out the door, climbing the side gutter and vanishing onto the rooftop. Moments later, he reappeared, howling and his arms were flailing helplessly, trying to cool the burn. He drifted across the rooftop, leaping from house to house in a frenzied path, leaving disarray and a vile stench in his wake. He was able to dart through the air, hurdle above and then ferociously burrow into the ground in seconds, only to resurface again— over and over—repeating his ups and downs, all the while, he shrieked, "Have mercy! Ouch! Have mercy!"

When I later returned to inspect the damage left behind in the garden, the stench was unbearable. He had even left a large stain on the neighbor's lawn, tearing up the grass as he galloped past their roof, like a Tasmanian devil marking his territory.

For the next month, I cleaned the mess Megalomiti had left behind, haunted by one question: Why did he invade my home? Worse, I was concerned I might have caught some disease from this wretched creature. Out of caution, I isolated myself for two weeks.

I couldn't shake the thought, maybe all he wanted was carrot juice. If I had just offered it to him, perhaps things would have gone differently. Yet, I feared his every uninvited move. He was malicious, and I prayed he would never return.

# The Kalikantzaroi — A Christmas Tale

# Beginnings

So, you are probably wondering...who was this mischievous goblin? He is known as a *Kalikantzaros* (or *Kalikantzaroi* for plural). Have you heard of them?

These sprites originated from ancient Greek times, particularly from the Anatolian area of Greece. The imp resembles the form of an elf or a gnome—which you may be familiar with. However, these Kalikantzaroi are far more sinister. If you ever encounter one, heed my advice and warning: never entertain a Kalikantzaros. They are evil, and delight in tormenting their victims.

Here's the thing about the Kalikantzaroi, they're not just mischievous; they're malevolent. They make evil choices. These chaotic spirits emerge from the bowels of the earth during the Twelve Days of Christmas, from December 25$^{th}$ to January 6$^{th}$.

Coincidentally, this is when the sun's light is at its weakest. Their goal? To wreak havoc on the world above. In their spare time, they gnaw away at the Tree of Life, hoping to bring about its collapse—and with it, doom for all.

In Turkish, they are known as *Karakoncolos*. "*Kara*" means black, and "*koncolos*" refers to a bloodsucking werewolf. I'm serious! These dark, purplish, scruffy creatures hide beneath the earth's surface for most of the year, and then appear just for a short time.

At least the Greeks softened the name to **Kali**kantzaros, derived from the words "*Kalos kentauros*," meaning "beautiful centaur"—half man, half horse. But don't let the name fool you. Kalikantzaroi are not to be trifled with. They thrive on madness and will leave your life in ruins.

This tragopod resembles a short, goat-footed, werewolf-like creature. The small lycanthrope has two caprine legs and wags its foot-long tail for balance and tactile-visual acuity—since they struggle to see in the brightness when surfacing the earth. It's dark beneath land, so they use their tails to help keep themselves grounded—sort of like a third arm and hand.

My doctor believes these creatures suffer from hypertrichosis—a rare condition that causes excessive hair growth. But, that doesn't explain why their two legs resemble those of a mare! What do doctors know about these creatures anyway? They've never seen one up close, like I have.

As I've mentioned, they only appear above the earth's surface during the twelve days of Christmas. The sun is rarely visible during the winter solstice, a time when these rascals become a troubling nuisance for humans. While the yuletide spirit pleasantly carries on with Christmas, these goblins creep about in the shadows, causing trouble before disappearing back to the center of the earth.

I believe they are intent on dismantling the Tree of Life.

These wretched souls are not your friendly neighborhood elves or gnomes. Oh no! They are grotesque, stunted beings, two-legged, sometimes single-hooved (though a few are double-hooved), with dark-purplish skin. All of the ones I've encountered are males, covered head-to-toe in hair. They balance themselves with their long and curled tails—tails seemingly designed by the Devil himself, which help them spring back to their feet.

They walk with agility and run as fast as ostriches. I've seen three bearing tusks, like those of a boar. Another three were unnaturally large, but most are tiny creatures, ranging from pocket-sized to about two feet tall. And they reek, carrying a stench of decay so abhorrent, it defies description.

Those dysfunctional blood-red eyes can barely withstand daylight, likely due to their life in the dark subterranean depths. Some people mistake them for elves because of their pointed ears, but Kalikantzaroi are different, they have propeller-shaped ears that resemble a goat, with huge heads, and their tongues hang out of their mouths, drooling mid-air, perhaps a way to regulate their body temperature.

They fear anything that involves light—whether physical or spiritual. This includes fire and, of course, holy water. I always keep a small bottle of holy water at home, just in case I need to sprinkle it around to disturb their comfort zone and force them to flee.

They sustain their unruly lives by gorging mainly on insects, and other decomposed organic matter. During winter's darkest days, they crawl out from their underground lairs eager to feast on these insects, trash, and spoiled food. They savor the taste of moist earthy worms, moles, grubs, snails and I've even seen one swallow a frog in one bite; the frog's legs still pulsed, attempting to swim or escape out of the creature's mouth, as it was devoured whole. The Kalikantzaros smiled at me as he gulped the poor amphibian down.

Once inside a home, they can cause all sorts of havoc, and are difficult to get rid of. They hide in basements, within the home walls, and even inside the masonry. They slip through the cracked doors, open keyholes, and chimneys; occasionally, making it through a loose window frame.

So, why don't I fear them? I probably should, but I've dealt with these creatures my entire life because, well, my name is Christopher Kringle, and you likely know me as Santa Claus!

Yes, these little critters tried to ruin Christmas for me a long time ago, but they weren't very bright. Annoying, yes, but I know how to handle them. In the beginning, they were voracious pests.

I encountered my first Kalikantzaros while sliding down a family chimney. He was scurrying back and forth; shifting side-to-side of the chimney flue! His tail snagged my long hat, and then, the rascal nibbled at my boots! Little did this tiny demon know that my boots were made of thick leather, not exactly a snack. They weren't edible! I grabbed the creature and flung it out of the chimney. Within seconds, my reindeer handled the rest. I think they processed the tiny fellow, and that was the end of that!

Over the past four hundred years, I've come across several of these pests, but they've never been able to stop Christmas. These critters aren't that smart, and are hardly successful at anything—except to eat ground meal, and to hack away at the Tree of Life. They are preoccupied with harmful behaviors, which results in nothing but trouble.

I will share a few more stories about these creepy demons, and the games they play. Once you learn to identify them, you'll understand why they've never made it onto my Nice List. The Kalikantzaroi are mischievous and bothersome. I don't believe they mean any harm, but they sure know how to stir up trouble! Their destructive deeds can damage your home and cause plenty of frustration.

*"Lord Jesus Christ,
　　　Son of God,
　　have mercy on me,
　　　　　a sinner."*

If you suspect one lurking around, keep an eye out and say the Jesus Prayer often—they despise it. Call upon divine protection to ward off these little demons: *"Lord Jesus Christ, Son of God, have mercy on me."*

To date, we've only identified about twenty of these creatures, though rumors say there are thousands more. I'll tell you about the ones I've encountered, so you will know immediately what to look for. And, maybe, just maybe, you can stop them from causing further naughtiness. If nothing else, you'll learn what not to do. These are creatures of the night, preying on despair. Be vigilant, stay safe, and be aware of what might be lurking in the shadows.

Now, let me tell you the story of the Kalikantzaroi...

# The Legend Develops

One of the worst Kalikantzaroi I've ever encountered was Katahanas. A gluttonous creature with an insatiable appetite, he would devour anything in sight. He ate and ate, and ate and ate. One year he developed a twisted obsession with chewing through the wooden beams of my home. Every night, I'd hear the ominous creaking of the foundation as he gnawed away, threatening to bring the entire structure crashing down! He was relentless. I finally sprinkled salt, cinnamon and baking soda around the foundation, and that put an end to his chewing. Although, he simply moved to the yard, where he slurped up grubs from under the grass yard. The smell he produced was horrible, and as flies gathered around him, his long tongue would swish up the nearest fly and he'd curl it in.

He did the same with crickets, snatching them like a lizard.

Something strange I noticed, and most disturbing, was the way his head and body shifted from side to side, moving even faster than his tongue! He wanted to gather as many grubs from the earth. He thrust his head into the grass and dirt, squeezing out the wet mud, and bursting the sluggish larva forward, swallowing the gelatinous blobs. It was rather a disgusting spectacle. Katahanas wasn't just a menace, he was a living wrecking ball, determined to feast on destruction through his endless hunger.

On another encounter with Katahanas, it was not his gluttony that caused trouble, instead he wielded the power of illusions. Casting a mirage in order to deceive and mislead. One Christmas night, he conjured a vision of a warm, inviting cottage, positioned in the middle of a dark forest.

The illusion lured in not only lost travelers deep within the woods, but also unsuspecting St. Nicholas! I followed those flickering lights, and soon became trapped in a maze of thorny wild berry bushes and evergreen branches. Our cries echoed through the cold night as we all suffered cuts and scratches from the thorns. By the time dawn broke, we managed to find our way out, though we were all exhausted and now fully aware of the treacherous tricks lurking in Katahanas' shadow. I almost missed delivering Christmas presents that year!

He wasn't alone in his mischief, his chum, Magáras, was just as troublesome. With a swollen belly filled with putrid gas, his smell was unbearable, like inhaling poison. His most devious talent was mimicry. He could imitate any sound, perfectly, using only his voice.

One night, he howled like a wolf, frightening all the children and livestock. On another incident, he imitated the village alarm sound, the loud bell clanging, and it was all just from his voice! It sent the villagers into panic, as they searched for the fire that didn't exist. While they were distracted by this imaginary emergency, Magáras slipped into their homes, overturning furniture and ripping down curtains. The residents spent days restoring town order, bewildered and wondering how easily they had been deceived by the clever brute.

I once saw Magáras wobble past Katahanas, and snatch the last cricket in the yard. Together they wreaked havoc. I remember how Magáras opened their conversation, grumbling, "I'm exhausted. I tried sleeping earlier, but Zena wouldn't let me rest for even fifteen minutes. Just for that, I'm going to tear through the house and wreck their furniture!"

True to his word, he clambered onto the couch, tossing pillows everywhere, before dashing around the room and banging into everything in sight. He broke furniture as he went, leaving behind an odor of rot and mold on everything he touched. The deliberate chaos they created was unbearable, and their destructive antics still haunt me.

On another day, his buddy Dolios stepped forward with a sly grin, "Look at me! Watch this, I'm going to convince that little girl outside to drop her candy, and then I'll have it all to myself!" He dashed past the other scoundrels, sprinted outside, and zipped toward the girl standing on the front sidewalk. With a quick pinch at her feet, he stared her down, his beady red eyes gleaming. The girl, frozen in horror, let out a terrified yelp!

"Ahh! Get away from me!" she screamed, jumping back and dropped her candy bar in her panic. She turned and ran for safety, screaming and gasping for air along the way. "A Kalikantzaros! A Kalikantzaros!" She had heard the warnings from her parents about the little beasts, and knew exactly what it was. Dolios sneered, then gathered up his loot of half-eaten chocolate, walked back with a smirk on his face, and brushed aside his hairy beard. He began to nibble on the chocolate when suddenly Katahanas pounced on him, yanking the treat from his hand and devoured it in one chomp.

Dolios spun around, but instead of getting upset at Katahanas, he barked out, "I was bringing it for you, anyway." Then, he spotted another girl walking by outside, and this time he changed tactics. He approached her directly, eyeing and asking her for anything in her lunch bag. "If you've got meat or bread in there, I'd like that…"

The girl marveled at the look of the creature, she was more curious than scared. In bewilderment, she slowly pulled out her school lunch sandwich, yet after a brief hesitation, quickly decided to give him the entire lunch bag. She stood calmly and wasn't frightened, but instead, was puzzled at the grotesque site. Without a word, she watched Dolios inspect it. A moment later, he turned and hopped away, pulling out the pieces he wanted and tossing the rest in all directions, leaving behind a trail of crumbs and wrappers.

What was fascinating about Dolios was that he actually knew how to read and write, although only at about the fifth-grade level. He forged letters, deceiving people with false promises, and for others he issued phony letters with dire warnings. Each letter he created sowed distrust amongst the neighbors, and each letter falsely warned of the other villager's fearful endeavor.

He created suspicion amongst them all, but then, his scheme began to unravel when the local police, who happened to be two brothers, discovered several identical letters, each addressed to different people. They pieced together the emerging inaccuracies and realized there were no truths in the letters, just manipulative fabrication. Saving the town from further damage to their relationships.

Then came Koutsos, the most dangerous of them all, who appeared just as Dolios entered the house. Koutsos was the chief of the clan, also the shortest and stockiest. I must say, he was the nastiest, clumsiest and most vicious of the Kalikantzaroi. His real name was Mantrakoúkos, he was an immoral and violent beast. They also called him "Protos" for short, meaning *first*.

His only pleasure was tormenting humans, mocking their attempts to ward him off. As Koutsos shuffled forward with his stocky clubbed feet, he boasted how he would harass the neighborhood at night. He especially loved tormenting women; teasing them, stealing their belongings, and raiding their refrigerators.

"Why do they even put food in those ice boxes?" he sneered. "Don't these humans know that spoiled meat is more tender and easier to digest?"

Koutsos could eat an entire ribeye steak, and liked it raw!

What Koutsos craved most were large bones, they were his delicacy. He would split them lengthwise, and like a canoe, he'd bore out the soft, buttery-fat marrow. His tongue would noisily scoop up the creamy substance, followed by a loud slurp.

"The marrow is the best part!" he'd declare with pride. Strangely enough, people seem to agree with him now. Perhaps it was feasting on that rich marrow that made this cantankerous fellow roar like a lion, and delight in scaring others for amusement.

Recently, however, Koutsos developed a newfound bizarre obsession with dirt and fire. Unlike the others, he seemed fearless around flames. He would set haystacks ablaze, then scatter dirt everywhere, creating swirling dust clouds that either spread or smothered the fire.

It didn't matter to him; he just loved the sight of dust mingling with the flames. Even the bucket brigade struggled to put out the fires, as Koutsos would either steal their water buckets or pack them with clay dirt, forcing the firefighters to stop and clean out the mess before refilling.

The scorched earth and scars left in his wake were a constant reminder of Koutsos and his malevolence.

Koutsos exited the house as quickly as he had entered, and no one knew where he was headed, but they would hear about his "achievements" of cruelty later, as the town complained with sour details of his misdeeds. He cherished the night and hid during the day.

The only "nice" Kalikantzaros, if one could call him that, was Kopsomesitis. He seemed half pleasant and never caused any real troubles; he doesn't destroy things. Instead, he simply moves items around, as a prank. While less harmful, it was still disruptive and unsettling to our peace. You understand how this can be annoying; if he took something you really needed at that moment. He would gather items, stack them over his hunched back, and walk for miles until he grew tired, then he'd leave them somewhere for another person to find. Sometimes, these items made their way back to their rightful owners, but often they didn't.

It was kind of a playful game for Kopsomesitis.

Many packages, letters, and shipments went undelivered—or ended up at the wrong addresses. The resulting confusion strained people's patience. It forced tempers to be controlled, and complicated even simple tasks.

Then, every night, he'd dive into some pancake batter and devour it, with a load of honey. His favorite treat was Greek loukoumades, a delight all of them enjoyed. These small, round donuts are made from a special batter, fried to perfection, and topped with honey, cinnamon and crushed walnuts. They are yummy—irresistible, in fact. It's nearly impossible to stop at just one.

This is one of their secret weaknesses: these goblins can't resist sweets.

Preparing a batch of loukoumades is a tried-and-true way to get rid of the Kalikantzaroi. If you leave some out, they'll be too busy eating to cause trouble. No one can resist these donuts, and for the Kalikantzaroi, it's a particular weakness. The sweetness melts their hearts, and they leave the home undisturbed.

I once saw the devilish Malaperda, he was galloping in the kitchen, knocking things over and thrashing at the pots and pans. When he came across an uncovered dish of food, he wasted no time plunging his filthy fingers into the food! Disgusting. This is why Malaperda is infamous for playing with food—and often while it is still being baked or cooked! Thus, you should always remember to close the lid on your pot, because of this crude habit of Malaperda.

# The Kalikantzaroi — A Christmas Tale

What was most fascinating, and frightening, is Malaperda's ability to manipulate the elements. Somehow, he could summon gusts of wind for example, to snuff out the candles, and would leave a home in total darkness. I've seen him uproot a tree, with a single gust of wind, leaving behind the daunting task of replanting, while trying to understand how these unexpected disasters had struck.

And then, the varmint lingered just long enough to leave behind the obscenest stench imaginable—a true travesty. The next day, a kind mother of three walked into her kitchen, devastated by the sight and smells left by the pesky Malaperda. Still, she couldn't help but blame herself for leaving the lid open.

It reminded her of years past, when another derelict named Koloveloni, a silent-stepping thief, had crept into her home, stole every piece of her clothing from the house and dragged them outside. Leaving them soiled and beyond saving or even repair. Koloveloni would also gnaw through sacks of flour and grain, contaminating them, and in the harshness of winter, when survival depended on stored provisions, it put the people into further hardship. As a result, people had to learn to ration what little they had, or replenish what was lost. All because of the sabotaging Koloveloni.

Koloveloni could slither through the tiniest holes and crevices, he was an expert at crawling under a door jam and passing through the threshold with ease. As a fast-moving creature, thin and long, he moved like a snake.

Back then, the mother blamed herself, because she left her clothes on the couch and chair in the bedroom, instead of hanging them up at the end of the day. Had she been more organized, they might have escaped Koloveloni's grasp, as he only disturbed what lay in his immediate view. She crossed herself and prayed to the good Lord for mercy.

This brings me to possibly my "favorite" Kalikantzaros, who is known as Paroritis. He has talents, but he misuses them. What a loss to the world. With his extraordinarily long nose, extending like an elephant's trunk with a rounded tip, Paroritis could smell everything. He could also create different sounds and mimic people's speech better than the smartest parrot. I had held out some hope for him, but it was lost once I saw all the damage he caused. Paroritis was an inflammation. An irritant, he created mountains of trouble wherever he went.

The worst was his morning rampage through a home, that upset all the animals and sent them into a frenzy. Chickens dashed frantically from wall to wall, the dogs barked and howled at the early morning dew. Even the pet gerbil, usually silent, was let out strange hissing noises, when it would never make a peep!

Then, in a swift leap, Paroritis jumped on the kitchen table, grabbed all the honey and a bag of sugar, and jolted out of the home.

Honey dripped in sticky lines behind him, and he dust and tossed sugar into the air, gulping spoonfuls while it fell with gravity into his mouth—and all over the floor and walls.

The mess he left behind compounded with the stench from his dirty hooves and matted hair, and created a nauseating state in that kitchen. The sheer disregard he showed, not only for humans, but for everything that stood in his way, turned the home into a disaster zone. He's a master at turning order into turmoil.

The family had to hand-washed everything, from ceiling to the floor, scrubbing with soap and water for days.

Paroritis didn't stop at making physical messes. He would also whisper nightmares into the ears of sleeping children. They would wake up screaming from visions of monsters, and the adults would also be haunted by fears of famine and loss. The fatigue from worry and sleepless nights eroded their spirits, making them irritable and angry, or worse, take out their troubles on one another, in the form of quarrels. It was all Paroritis' doing, planting the terrible thoughts in their minds like seeds of misery.

Occasionally, this unseen menace made mistakes, and people would catch him in the act. While it brought a glimmer of hope, the real victory was in sharing their stories with their neighbors and friends. In doing so, they found comfort in each other, slowly restoring their morale.

During one of the harshest snow seasons in recorded history, I found myself lost in the mountains of northern Greece. The houses were tightly shuttered, desperate to retain what little warmth they could. It was there, amid the bitter cold, that I confronted Katsipodiaris.

In Greek, "katsika" means *goat*, and "podi" means *foot*. As I've stated before, he earned his name due to the unmistakable appearance of his goat-like feet. While many of these creatures share similar traits, Katsipodiaris was one of the first to be identified, cementing his name as the "Goat Foot." Katsipodiaris is lazy, to put it mildly. He's also the most miserable and ill-mannered of the Kalikantzaroi, constantly rubbing his bald head until it is buffed and shimmering like a polished stone.

Have you heard of people driven for success? Well, Katsipodiaris is driven for disaster! He is the sonorous catastrophe! He disrupts all communication. As the embodiment of calamity, everything he touches becomes destroyed. For him, it's all a game, jumping from one consequence to another. The aftermath is irrevocable. Prayers for anyone who crosses paths with Katsipodiaris. I've seen firsthand the so-called "work" he's done, and let me tell you, there's no silver lining. He has a way of meddling in people's affairs, never for their benefit, and the outcome is usually irreversible damage.

There are others of his kind, but I haven't encountered them myself—yet. Like Kopsacheilis, for instance, who apparently has massive teeth that hang grotesquely over his lips. They say he mocks the clergy, ridiculing our faith and even desecrating sacred relics. He once overturned an altar, simply because the candles were too bright for his liking. I've heard stories of him dressing in priestly robes and donning a bishop's hat, trying to pass himself off as clergy and misdirect people. Except, he could never conceal his goat legs for long, nor his lack of spiritual knowledge.

Most of the folks are deeply rooted in their faith, and they found him violating, genuinely appalled by his mockery. In the end, the real priest organized a vigil, and all the members of the church cleansed the chapel area, restoring it to a place of peace and unwavering devotion.

## The Season

As Christmastime unfolds, these critters grow increasingly agitated. Their devious activities intensify as our awareness of the world's blessings deepens. We sing hymns, share uplifting stories of courage and kindness, and fill the air with the scent of incense, and the sounds of joy and laughter. Frightened by this, they let out shrieks before they vanish from sight, not to return until the next year.

This brings us to why it's important to protect ourselves against these critters. Many inscribe blessings on doorways, while others hang herbs or special candles that burn through the night, all meant to ward off the darkness.

Some say that placing sage (or a protective charm like a horseshoe, or I prefer a religious icon) in a doorstep at night will keep evil at bay. Others sprinkle holy water. Many mark their doors with a cross on the Eve of Christmas, preparing for these demons and blocking their interference. What seems to work best, however, is when families gather in the evening to share a meal. This reinforces the family bond, drawing strength from one another.

After Christmas Eve, as the Kalikantzaroi grow bolder, so does the people's resolve. Burning logs in the fireplace helps too. The smoke and heat from the chimney keep them away, at least until they disappear again back to the center of the earth.

It all leads to a festive climax on January 6th, with the celebration of the Epiphany, and the houses are all blessed with sanctified water sprinkled from fresh bundles of basil, known as the king's herb. This day commemorates and reminds us of the visit of the three Magi to infant Jesus, bringing gifts of myrrh and ointments. We celebrate this birth of Christ. Even the word "epiphany" comes from the Greek language, meaning "the reveal" or what one can consider the "revelation."

Epiphany! It is that sense of great enlightenment—the "Aha!" moment—and quite simply, a miracle. The Kalikantzaroi are powerless against the strength of the community that unites in faith during this time. Their solidarity dwindles in the face of such hope. This is why it's so important to stand together, keep the light of kindness burning bright, and face the darkness without fear.

## The Kalikantzaroi — A Christmas Tale

Some have asked me, "Are they the same as leprechauns or figures from Irish folklore?" I can only say, no—not at all. Because of a few reasons. For one, these little Kalikantzaroi speak mainly English and Greek. Their appearance is quite different too; Kalikantzaroi are filthy and shaggy, and have legs far more grotesque than the more human-like leprechauns. Everything about them is different—how they function, eat, live in the darkness, and go about their terrible ways.

Have you heard of the World Tree or the Tree of Life? It is the colossal tree that supports and connects the universe; our heaven, with the earth and the underworld. Every year, when these goblins see that it has grown again, they get busy, trying to cut it down at the trunk! It's terrible. Then, the tree begins to heal itself, and then the cycle happens again. Thankfully, the Tree of Life has continued to grow, and despite their efforts for destruction, it continues to thrive, especially during those few short days when we become more aware of its existence.

So, don't forget to make a batch of loukoumades during the holidays! Leave a few on your rooftop, throw them up there if you can't reach! I've also heard they love sausages, so that might help, or perhaps, leaving one out in the kitchen will do the trick to send them away.

Despite their chaos, the Kalikantzaroi fear one thing above all: goodness. Prayers can drive them back underground. They can't bear to see the light, whether physical or spiritual. So, during the Twelve Days of Christmas, when they try to portray a time of "power," remember that the tables will turn. The blessed waters that sanctify our homes will push these goblins back to their underworld in fear.

Why am I not afraid? Because I'm Christopher Kringle, and I've been dealing with them for centuries. They've tried to interfere with my life and work, but their tricks are powerless against kindness, generosity, and faith. You see, the Kalikantzaroi thrive on chaos and despair, but they wither in the presence of joy and goodness.

Reflecting on the behavior of these creatures, there are moral lessons we can learn from them—reminders that even in the midst of their wickedness, we can find goodness.

## The Kalikantzaroi — A Christmas Tale

# The Takeaway

So, what can we learn from the Kalikantzaroi? As someone who admires a good list, let's take a moment to reflect on the lessons hidden within their mischief:

1. **Chaos never has lasting power.**

    While havoc may cause harm and suffering, eventually, goodness always rises above it.

2. **Goodness always prevails.**

    Just as the Kalikantzaroi may attempt to deceive and outwit others, like all evil forces try to overpower, they cannot endure when met with goodness and wisdom.

## 3. Light overcomes darkness.

Just as truth and virtue, like light, dispel darkness and ignorance, embracing what is true and good is your best defense against unruliness. The light always finds a way to shine through. Darkness has no staying power when confronted with light.

## 4. Mischief has consequences!

The callous acts of the Kalikantzaroi—spreading fear, destroying homes, and disrupting peace—have serious consequences. Their recklessness teaches us that thoughtless actions always come with a price.

5. **People show resilience in the face of adversity.**

   Although the annoyances and devastation can feel constant and never ending, good people endure. They remain calm, push forward, and persist in the face of challenges; standing strong even when life seems overwhelming. We adapt and find ways to persevere.

6. **Deception breeds distrust.**

   Just as Dolios deceived others with false letters, dishonesty fractures trust, leading to suspicion and strife. Trust, once broken, is difficult to rebuild. This is why we begin with the truth, always keep our integrity and act courageously. We should stand for what is right and go against what is wrong. This is the cornerstone and foundation of healthy relationships.

7. **Spirituality is a shield against difficulty.**

    Faith, prayer and spiritual discipline offer protection against unruliness and evil. Never abandon your faith and values. They are your anchor in turbulent times.

8. **Respect others' space and property.**

    The destructive nature of the Kalikantzaroi (stealing, invading, and vandalizing) reminds us of the importance of honoring other's belongings and personal space. This upholds peace, helps maintain societal order, and builds mutual respect.

9. **Greed leads to destruction.**

 Characters like Katahanas, driven by gluttony and unchecked desires, bring ruin to the people and surroundings around them. This warns us to keep our cravings in check, so they don't spiral out of control.

10. **Kindness can tame even the worst troublemakers.**

 Though the Kalikantzaroi are malicious, they can be swayed by goodness. Compassion and understanding can diffuse hostility and bring about transformation, even in the darkest of hearts.

And that, my friend, is the true lesson of this tale. The Kalikantzaroi may be terrifying, but their power only lasts as long as we allow them to disrupt our lives. By holding onto light, love, and compassion, we can ensure their darkness never prevails.

So, this holiday season, if you hear the scampering of little feet or catch a whiff of something foul in the air, don't be afraid. Light a candle, say a prayer, and extend a helping hand to those in need. For, in the end, goodness always triumphs over evil.

Have a Merry Christmas, stay vigilant, cherish your loved ones, and let your acts of kindness shine brightly!

# The Kalikantzaroi — A Christmas Tale

NIKOS LINARDAKIS

*Notes*

*Notes*

## Notes

Made in the USA
Columbia, SC
22 November 2024